Thomas Bulfinch

The Boy Inventor

A memoir of Matthew Edwards, mathematical-instrument maker

Thomas Bulfinch

The Boy Inventor
A memoir of Matthew Edwards, mathematical-instrument maker

ISBN/EAN: 9783744742955

Printed in Europe, USA, Canada, Australia, Japan

Cover: Foto ©Raphael Reischuk / pixelio.de

More available books at **www.hansebooks.com**

L.Grezellers Lith

A Book for Young Men.

THE BOY INVENTOR;

A MEMOIR OF

MATTHEW EDWARDS,

MATHEMATICAL-INSTRUMENT MAKER.

"To scorn delights and live laborious days."
MILTON.

BOSTON:
WALKER, WISE, & CO.,
245 WASHINGTON STREET.
1860.

University Press, Cambridge:
Electrotyped and Printed by Welch, Bigelow, & Co.

TO THE

MECHANIC APPRENTICES' LIBRARY ASSOCIATION,

THIS MEMOIR

IS RESPECTFULLY DEDICATED.

PREFACE.

THE first part of this Memoir was written more than two years ago, and intended as a contribution to a juvenile magazine. This will account for its juvenile tone. When written, it was laid aside; the idea of its publication being relinquished, from a fear that the effect might be injurious to the youth whose adventures it relates. That fear being removed by the sad event of his death, the Memoir, with additions, completing the brief story, is given to the public, in the hope that it may awaken kind sentiments and quicken good impulses in the breasts of readers, whether youthful or more mature.

T. B.

CONTENTS.

THE BOY INVENTOR.

CHAPTER I.

BIRTH AND EARLY LIFE.

THE young man to whom these pages relate was known to not a few of the citizens of Boston for his engaging personal qualities and his noble efforts for self-improvement. It is thought a brief record of his career may be useful in showing how much may be accomplished by an unknown youth in a foreign land, by the diligent improvement of his opportunities; and how even a short life, if faithfully used, can leave a precious memory. Perhaps, too, the early close of this promising career may impart its lesson, teaching that every earthly object is to be pursued with moderation; and that the issue of our best-meant efforts rests, after all, with the great Disposer of events.

Matthew Edwards was born of honest but poor parents, in the town of Derby, England, on the 23d day of July, 1838. His father was a stocking weaver; and when stockings and small-clothes went out of fashion, he followed the business of collecting bills for his neighbors, by which he supported his family frugally, but comfortably. Matthew was the youngest child, and not much could be done for his schooling; for in England schooling is not free to all, but has to be paid for. Matthew made the best of his time, and learned to read, write, and cipher, and got a tolerable knowledge of geography.

At ten and a half years old he left school to go apprentice to a printer. One night there was a terrible storm, and next morning when they came to the office they found that the chimney had been blown over, and had fallen on the roof and crushed it into the printing-office, filling all with bricks and rafters. All hands immediately set to work to clear away the rubbish, some of the boys loading up others, who carried down the bricks and piled them in the yard. Matthew did his part manfully, but it was too hard work for him; and when he went home he was in pain all over, was restless all night, and next day was found to have a violent attack of acute rheumatism. This is a terrible complaint, which swells the joints and limbs, and renders one inca- pable of walking or using his hands, while the pain is very severe, and even lying in bed affords no relief. Matthew was so ill that he had to give up the printing-office, and it was nine months before he was able to undertake any kind of business.

While he was slowly recovering, he saw, one day, in a shop-window, a book standing open against the glass, with a picture unfolded, containing drawings of air-pumps, electrical-machines, &c., and he gazed at this picture, day by day, and read all that was printed on the picture and on the printed page. At last he went into the shop and inquired the price of the book, and was told *a shilling.* He had not money to buy it if it had been but half as much; but when he went home he told his mother how much he wished he could have that book. She could not venture to spend so much money merely to gratify a childish fancy, but said she would ask his father. The good man promised to go and look at the book. He did so, and told the bookseller the fancy his boy had for it, and asked him if he thought it was a good book; when a gentleman in the shop, overhearing the conversation, stepped forward and said it was a very good little book, and moreover, he added, "If my boy had any fancy for such a book, I should buy it for him with pleasure." So Matthew's father bought the book.

Matthew was now at the summit of happiness. He read all about the air-pump, the air-gun, the electrical-machine, the fire-engine, and many other things, spelling out the hard words as well as he could, and almost got his book by heart.

There was a shop which he passed sometimes where they made philosophical instruments, and in the windows were several machines placed to catch the eye of the passer-by. Matthew used to stand

and gaze at this window, till he thought if he could only get a glass cylinder he could make an electrical machine. He saved up his money till he had got enough (almost a dollar) to buy a cylinder, and then he went to work to prepare a cushion to rub it. The cushion is made of silk, and covered with an amalgam, or paste, made of quicksilver and tinfoil, rubbed together in a mortar. He made also a Leyden jar to receive the electricity. It is coated within and without with tinfoil. When he got his rubber ready, he rubbed his cylinder and charged his jar, and took off a shock, and gave one to his father and mother and the cat. Puss was persuaded to put her nose to the jar, and got what made her jump and run away.

In making his electrical machine, Matthew had frequent need to ask advice. There was no one at home to advise him, and he went to the man who kept the philosophical-instrument shop, and asked questions of him. The man soon got to know Matthew quite well, and one day asked him if he would

2

not like to come and be apprentice to him. Matthew liked the thought very much, and his father gladly accepted the offer. The custom in England is, for an apprentice entering a business of that kind, to pay an entrance fee; and at that shop the fee was a hundred and fifty dollars. But the gentleman consented to take Matthew without any fee.

Here he passed two years, till his elder brother got married, and made up his mind to seek his fortune in America. Matthew went with them, with the consent of his parents and his employer, and in the spring of 1853 landed in Boston. Here he was, a boy of fourteen and a half years old, with none to advise him except his brother and wife, strangers like himself, and having enough to do to make their own arrangements. He lost no time in inquiring out a maker of philosophical instruments, and presented himself at the shop, offering to come as an apprentice. He was accepted; and before the end of the first week after his arrival was at work for his new master. But he soon perceived that the kind of work done at that shop was not the highest branch of the art. The instruments made there were such as are used for school apparatus, which are as simple and cheap as possible; and Matthew thought if he only learned to make such as those, he should hardly be master of his trade. So he inquired if there was not in the town some manufacturer who made better instruments, and he found that there was. He applied to him, was accepted, and after two weeks' employment in his first place, removed to his second, where he remained to the end of his apprenticeship, five years.

His pay was enough to support him and leave a little over. He did not waste that little in idle gratifications, so that he laid up money slowly; and I will tell you by and by how he spent it.

During the greater part of the time that he was in this employment, Matthew did not fail to occupy his mind with some kind of study; but having no friend

to guide him, accident in some measure decided the
course of his studies.   He was smitten with a warm
admiration for public speaking, and it was the height
of his ambition to become an accomplished, orator.
He inquired what books there were on the subject,
and one was shown him, written by Dr. Rush of
Philadelphia, upon the Voice.   This is a work not
for a beginner, but for a mature and educated
reader.   But Matthew went to work upon it with
all his heart, and read it through and through
again, with admiration.   Not that he could understand it all, — far from it; but what he could understand seemed to him full of wisdom.   It con-
tained allusions to other books, some of which he
got and read with it; for instance, Shakespeare's
plays and Blair's Rhetoric.   Ten hours and a half
a day he gave to his trade, and another hour and a
half to his meals; but the evening and early morning allowed him still some hours each day for his
books.   He had succeeded in getting a room by himself, though a small one and very high up.   After

his day's work he ran home, washed his hands, ate his supper, and then skipped up to his attic, where he devoted himself to his dear books to a late hour. But with all his study he could not quite master Dr. Rush's work, and he felt a longing desire to ask some one to explain to him what he found too hard for his powers. But whom should he ask? He could think of no one but the author himself. He had learned that Dr. Rush was still living, and resided in Philadelphia. If he could but go there, he might see him, and learn from himself the best explanation of his precepts. This thought occupied his mind for months. He had laid up nearly fifty dollars, and this would be more than enough to carry him to Philadelphia and bring him back. He mentioned his wish to his employer, who treated it as an idle fancy. But the thought dwelt on Matthew's mind, and at last he persuaded his master to allow him a fortnight's vacation for the purpose.

Behold him then, with nearly his whole for-

2 *   B

tune in his pocket, starting for Philadelphia, — a
young pilgrim to the shrine of his cherished sage.
He stopped no longer in New York than was necessary to change boats, and from the wharf at
Philadelphia inquired his way directly to the phi-
losopher's door. He found it, and rung the bell.
"Is Dr. Rush at home?" "No." This was a
disappointment, and he turned slowly away. Something in the servant's manner led him to think that
perhaps the Doctor might be at home, but not
exactly at leisure to see a boy. Matthew next
inquired his way to the store of the bookseller
who had published Dr. Rush's work; and there,
being admitted into the counting-room, he told the
gentleman his purpose in coming to Philadelphia,
and his disappointment in his attempt to see the
Doctor. Mr. L., the publisher, promised to speak
for him, and told him to make another attempt in
the evening. Matthew did so, was admitted, and
was led into the Doctor's study, and found himself
face to face with one for whom he had long felt

the greatest veneration. He told his object. He had come from Boston to ask the Doctor to explain certain things in his book. "What are they?" said the Doctor. Matthew opened the book, and found the first place. The Doctor explained. The boy showed intelligence; he understood the explanation; he accepted it with delight. He turned to a second place. Here, too, the Doctor explained, illustrated, exemplified. Thus the evening passed away. The pupil's enthusiasm, so flattering to the instructor, and the instructor's kindness, so gratifying to the pupil, kept them from feeling weary, or noting the lapse of time. When they parted, it was three o'clock in the morning.

The good Doctor made Matthew come to him every evening while he stayed in Philadelphia; and as he was not a teacher of elocution himself, he gave him an introduction to a gentleman who was. Professor A. was as much interested in Matthew as Dr. R. had been, and both joined in

advising him, if he so earnestly desired to acquire
the art of elocution, to cultivate his mind, and
study language and literature.   But how should
he, employed as he was nearly the whole time in
his trade, and without money to pay teachers, get
the requisite instruction ?   Professor A. gave him,
when he left Philadelphia to return home, a letter
to Mr. B., a gentleman of Boston who had leisure
and was fond of books, and who he thought would
be pleased with Matthew's zeal for learning, and
would help him forward.   With many thanks to
his kind friends, Matthew took his leave, and returned home.

He lost no time in presenting his letter of introduction to Mr. B., who received him kindly, and
told him to call in the evening.   Matthew came,
and told all his adventures and plans to his new
friend.   Dr. R. and Professor A. had both ad-
vised him, as the most effectual way of disciplining
his mind and getting a knowledge of language, to
study Latin.   Mr. B. told him, if he would get a

Latin grammar, he would tell him what to study; and he might come, one evening in the week, and recite his lessons. Matthew accepted the offer with delight. He got his grammar, and went to work upon his first lesson. After his day's work was done, he hardly allowed himself time for his supper, and then went straight to his attic and to his grammar. In the morning he rose as soon as it was light, and went and walked round the Common, grammar in hand, repeating to himself. When the week came round, he presented himself at Mr. B.'s study, and recited a good long lesson, so well got as to show that he was in earnest. Mr. B. felt his interest in him increase; and when, week after week, Matthew presented himself regularly as the evening came, always furnished with a lesson well committed, generally of no trifling length, Mr. B. began to take as much pleasure in the evening meetings as the boy himself. Matthew soon got through his grammar, and felt ambitious to begin to translate. Viri Romæ is not the first

book usually put next to the grammar; but Matthew looked at its first sentences, and thought he
could manage it, and Mr. B. allowed him to try.
He found it pretty hard at first, having no school-
mates to consult with and ask questions of, as most
schoolboys have; but at the end of the week he
had succeeded in translating the first half page,
and he wrote off his translation in his best hand
and brought it to his kind instructor. Mr. B. ex-
amined it, and said it was very well for a first
attempt, but not free from faults; and Matthew
took as much interest in having the faults pointed
out, and seeing how he had been led into them, as
he had taken in the translating itself. The next
lesson showed he had not forgotten the corrections
and instructions which he received upon his former
one, and every succeeding lesson showed more or
less improvement.

After the Latin lesson, it was Mr. B.'s plan to
devote the rest of the evening to hearing Matthew
read. This had a double advantage; it improved

the reading faculty, and it conveyed information. As India was then the reigning topic, they chose Macaulay's account of Lord Clive and of Warren Hastings, under whom the British empire in India . was established; and Matthew was so much interested, that he could hardly bear to lay down the book when ten o'clock came.

CHAPTER II.

MATTHEW IN 1858.

MATTHEW had now been four and a half years absent from his parents, and he wanted very much to go home to England and see them. His employer consented; but the expense was a serious obstacle. He thought he might possibly get a free passage in one of the steamers, in return for taking some care of the machinery. But he found that there was a regular establishment on board of each steamer for that duty, and no vacancy was to be found. However, by the help of kind friends, Matthew got permission to go free of charge, in return for making himself useful in any way in which he might be called upon. It resulted in his tending table at the officers' mess.

This was not an occupation very much to Matthew's taste; but he did his duty in it, and gave satisfaction. Among the passengers in the cabin was Professor W. B. Rogers. Mr. B. had given Matthew a letter of introduction to this gentleman, and the Professor was very kind to him, and took occasion several times to converse with him. This acquaintance was afterwards very valuable to Matthew. He spent a month in England, where he had the happiness of seeing his parents and other relatives in good health, and of renewing his intercourse with the friends of his childhood. In the early autumn he returned to Boston.

On his return he recommenced his labors at Mr. Temple's shop, and his weekly visits to Mr. B.'s chamber. His Latin studies went on finely; he showed a ready apprehension of the peculiarities of the language; few sentences were too hard for him, and it was not easy to puzzle him in parsing. The English readings were also continued. After Macaulay's Historical Essays on India,

3

his friend took up with him the History of the Spanish Conquest in South America, and after that, Young's Chronicles of the Pilgrim Founders of New England.

Matthew was rigorously self-exacting. He rose very early, and, after a walk, devoted himself to study. When cold weather came on, he still continued his early walks, often before light, and studied in his chamber, both morning and evening, without a fire. This was very imprudent, but he did it, as he said, to harden himself. He persevered in this practice all winter; but it was too much for his strength. In the early spring he had an attack of rheumatism. All at once his ankles and wrists swelled, so that he could neither walk nor labor, and was obliged to give up his work at the shop. After two weeks, getting no better, Mr. B. had him taken to the Massachusetts General Hospital, where he knew he would have the best of attendance. It was several weeks before Matthew got well enough to go out; and when he did he was still too feeble to labor. A kind friend proposed to him to go with him to the country, where he could have his board in return for such services as he could render on the farm. He accepted the offer, and went to Barrington, a farming town near Dover, N. H.

Here he was in a line of life new to him. He had never in his life mounted a horse. Here it was one of his duties to ride the horse that drew the harrow. This suited him exactly; and now and then he had the chance of riding some miles to do an errand. He made himself useful in various ways; he churned the butter, drew the water, and helped make hay. His part was to mount the load, and receive the hay when it was passed up on the pitchfork, and stow it carefully. It is quite a nice matter to stow a load of hay. For if it is not evenly laid on, but leans one side or the other, it will be likely to slide off, when the load is all packed, and give the labor to do over again. Matthew made himself very popular with the country boys and girls, for he was a good hand at a frolic, and made more fun than any one else. But he did not use all his time in working or frolicking. Mr. B. had lent him some books, which Matthew read when he could have an hour to himself. He read during this summer, Goldsmith's History of Rome twice through, Paley's Natural Theology, which is a charming book for an inquiring mind, though the title would lead one to think it must be too serious to be agreeable; he also read the Conversations on Chemistry, which gave him the groundwork of a science the knowledge of which was afterwards of great use to him.

In October he came back to Boston quite well. He returned to his work and his studies. This autumn he read parts of Gibbon's History of Rome, including the account of Mahomet, the founder of the Mahometan religion, and the narrative of the conquest of Constantinople by the Turks. He also read several of Plutarch's Lives of illustrious Greeks and Romans. But nothing interested him so much as Grote's Life of Socrates. This is a book which would, by those who read mainly for amusement, be called very dry reading, but it suited Matthew's taste. What that taste was may be inferred from another incident. When he was getting over his attack of illness, Mr. B. gave him The Vicar of Wakefield to read. He enjoyed it much. Next followed the story of Rasselas, and this pleased him more than the other. While he was in the country, he read Goldsmith's Traveller and Deserted Village, committing great part of them to memory. He also got by heart Gray's Elegy and Ode on Eton College. He preferred Goldsmith's to all other poetry he had read. He made that the standard. Other poetry was good in proportion as it approached that. His friend read him Scott's battle in Marmion. He did not relish it; he had no taste for tales of war and bloodshed. Milton's Comus and L' Allegro and Il Penseroso were read to him, but his taste was yet too immature to appreciate them

3 *

justly. Last of all, they read selected portions of
the famous romance of Don Quixote; and Matthew, who laughed as heartily as he labored, enjoyed highly the fun of Sancho and Dapple, while
he appreciated the generous and noble qualities of
the Don.

Thus passed the year 1858, and with that year
Matthew's apprenticeship ended. He was twenty
and a half years old; and now at last he felt he
had reached the time when he should receive full
wages, and be able to lay up money fast, to pay his
way through college. For his views had expanded.
as his education proceeded. He no longer limited
his ambition to being a public speaker, or even a
great actor, — an idea which once had charms for
him. He loved his calling, and felt no desire to
forsake it. But he aspired to be also a well-
educated man. No limit short of the possible
seemed to satisfy him. He would go to Harvard
College, and then to Germany, where he had
been told they carried their researches in every

path of learning further than was done anywhere else.

But Matthew found a difficulty in realizing his plans at the outset. His employer did not want a new journeyman. So Matthew went to another establishment, where he readily got employment on his own terms. But here the work was coarse, it was turned off in great haste, sufficiently well finished for the purposes for which it was intended, but not in the way in which Matthew had been taught to finish work. He feared he should soon lose in doing such work the delicacy of touch which he had been years in acquiring, and after staying two days he gave up his engagement.

He talked over his plans with his good friend. If he could but get a small shop and a few tools, he felt sure he might obtain work enough at repairing of instruments to pay as much or more than journeyman's wages. "How much will it cost?" was the inquiry. "Three hundred dollars would, perhaps, be enough." This was no great sum, and his friend readily undertook to supply it. So Matthew set himself the next day to find a work-room, and after examining several, selected one at No. 216½ Washington Street, where he found two small rooms, in the fourth story, looking out upon the street, the larger of which would do nicely for a shop, and the other for a bedroom and study. He got a friendly carpenter (everybody was friendly to Matthew) to put up his bench, attach his vise, and nail up slats, furnished with pins on which to hang his tools, fix him a box for his coal, and so forth. He procured a turning-lathe, the most complete that could be made, a small forge and an anvil, — not such an anvil as you see in blacksmiths' shops, but a little affair suited to the light work of his trade. He got an iron bedstead, of the kind which, when not in use, turns up against the wall, and, when covered with a curtain, hardly makes any show or takes up any room. He had a set of book-shelves, measuring about two feet square, in which stood all the books he had accumulated in his short life, from the little

Youth's Book of Amusement, which his mother bought for him in the beginning of his career, to Dr. Rush's work and Hudson's Shakespeare, his later acquisitions. Against the wall hung large daguerrotypes of his father and mother, brothers and sisters. His brother painted a sign for him, which he put up on the side of the entry door, — " Matthew Edwards, Mathematical-Instrument Maker," — and his establishment was now complete.

For two weeks not a single job offered. But Matthew was not idle. He had numerous tools to make; for in his business there are many required which are not for sale in the shops, and some of them are complicated. Before he had got through with them he received his first order, and then several others followed. One of the first was to make a model of a newly-invented instrument, to be sent to the Patent-Office at Washington. The drawings were supplied him, and he was to carry them into execution. How he succeeded, the following letter from his employer, when his work was sent home, will show.

C

Portland, July 3, 1859.

" Mr. M. Edwards : —

" Dear Sir, — I am happy to inform you that I
have received the machine safe; and many thanks
to you for the manner in which you have finished it.
But I am not able to tell you how the machine will
work yet, as there is some little fixing to be done
before I can try it.   But I am almost sure before-
hand that it will suit the purpose; but should it not,
there will be no blame on your part, as your work-
manship IS FIRST-RATE.

" You seem, in your letter, uneasy about your bill,
lest I think it too high.   I assure you I do not; and
should it ever be in my power, I will show you my
satisfaction with it in more material form than mere
words.

" I am, very sincerely, your well-wisher,

" THOS. JOHNSTON."

A few weeks after Matthew opened his shop, a
young man called upon him who was near finishing
his studies at the Scientific School at Cambridge.

He wished to procure an instrument used in survey-
ing, called a theodolite, the cost of which is about
three hundred dollars. He asked Matthew if he
could make him one. Matthew thought he could,
and referred his young customer to Mr. Temple
for information as to his ability. "I shall not make
any inquiry," said the student. "I can judge by
seeing." So Matthew undertook the theodolite.
You may see a picture of one in the new dictionary
of Dr. Worcester. When used, it is mounted on a
three-legged stand, called a tripod, which raises it to
the height of the observer's eye, to enable him to
look through the telescope which forms part of the
instrument.

Matthew had often heard surveyors complain of
this instrument, as usually constructed, that the levelling part worked badly. The levelling is effected by
screws, marked in the cut *K*, *L*, *P*. These screws,
when the instrument stands perfectly level, are perpendicular, but when the instrument is not perfectly
level, these screws have to be turned one way or the

other, to raise or depress the part to which they are attached. In this process they cease to be perpendicular, and operate in a slanting direction. This makes them work hardly; and as the usual resort of every one when a screw works hardly is to put on more force, the effect is often to bend the screws, or the plate to which they are fixed, thus spoiling the instrument.

Matthew thought he, could remedy this defect. He studied on it most intently. Here he found great benefit in consulting with his friend Professor Rogers, who had by this time returned, and renewed his acquaintance with Matthew. To make the screws always push in a perpendicular direction, Matthew saw that he must change the shape of the plate against which they press; it must not be a flat, but a curved surface. Now, what was this curve to be? He first tried a circle, but soon found it would not answer; for the screws which form the radii were at every turn lengthening or shortening, and the radius of a circle is of equal length in every part. Matthew concluded it must be an ellipse, and this was near enough right for all practical purposes. After designing his model, his next task was to make each separate part in wood, to form a mould in which the brass is to be cast to the required shape. After the castings are ready, the work of fitting and adapting each part to the others begins, and this is done with files of different degrees of fineness, the use of which is the great test of the workman's skill, and Matthew's fellow-workmen all say that in the use of the file none surpassed him.

It was a long task to do all this. The designing took a good while, and then each part had to be drawn on tin plates, for paper would not support the pressure of the compasses, where the points rest in taking measurements. Then the making of the patterns, all with extreme exactness, yet a little larger than the corresponding parts, to admit of filing down. All this preparation, it is evident, would serve, when once done, for ever so many

4

instruments after the first; but the first could not be made without it. It is therefore no wonder that Matthew's instrument advanced but slowly. He was so intent upon it that he refused all other jobs that offered, that he might devote himself to this.

While these labors were going on, Matthew prosecuted his studies. He translated from his Viri Romæ into English, and then, after two or three weeks' interval, put it back into Latin. He also took up Arnold's Latin Composition, a pretty difficult book, but he liked it all the better for that. He occasionally interrupted his Latin studies for a week or two, by the study of algebra, in which his good friend, Professor Rogers, assisted him. He never failed to spend his weekly evening with Mr. B., and after the Latin lesson they read together. Matthew read first; but as his eyes were not strong, Mr. B. took the book after a while. In this way he made acquaintance with Milton, Pope, Goldsmith, Gray, Scott, and Byron; a slight acquaintance indeed, but such that their names should not be to him mere names.

As the theodolite approached completion, his interest in it grew so engrossing that he gave up for a time his Latin and his algebra, but continued his evening readings. He also attended the Lowell Lectures, one course of which, by his friend, Professor Rogers, upon Air and Water, delighted him very much. Another good friend, Professor Bacon, of the Medical College, gave Matthew a ticket to his course of lectures on Chemistry. Two forenoons of each week, during the winter of 1859, Matthew turned the key on his shop and his instrument, and hasted away to the Medical College, where he enjoyed the advantage of hearing the admirable lectures of his friend, the Doctor, and of conferring with him on his own experiments.

Matthew was very social, and Mr. B. liked to have him vary his studies and labors by going into society. With this view he had introduced him into several domestic circles, where he would find appre-

ciating friends, and enjoy the benefit of female intercourse, so important to form the manners of a young
man. The circle was limited, for Matthew had not
much time to spare to it; but it was a source of
great happiness to him, and did for him what little
his natural courtesy required.

CHAPTER III.

ANECDOTES AND CONVERSATIONS.

EARLY in Matthew's acquaintance with Mr. B. he conceived the idea of going to College. Mr. B. told him there were helps afforded to young men like him, who aspired to gain a literary education, but whose means were limited. Matthew objected, "But I am an Englishman, and I do not wish to give up my country." "That makes no difference," replied his friend; "these funds were many of them given by Englishmen, and it would be hard if the fact of English birth should debar one from enjoying their benefits." Yet Matthew could not bring his mind to be aided pecuniarily. "I can earn the money," said he, "and I had rather do so." In the course of their conversations his friend mentioned

4 *

the case of one young man who had found the means of paying his way through college by insuring his life, and borrowing the money upon that security. Matthew inquired how this was done, and the conversation made an impression on his mind, though he did not act upon the idea at that time. But when, a year after, he found it necessary to borrow money to establish himself in business, he decided to get his life insured, as a security for his obligations. It was his own proposal, not suggested by any doubt or question on the part of the friend who aided him. The arrangement was made, and Matthew secured, by the payment of about twenty dollars a year, a thousand dollars, to be paid in case of his death. This took all burden off his mind, for he felt no doubt of his being able to pay all his borrowed money if he should live, and he now saw that even if he should not live to carry his plans into execution, those who trusted him would not lose their advances.

We have told candidly Matthew's attachment to

the name of Englishman, early in the term of his acquaintanceship with Mr. B., and that gentleman never by a word intentionally did anything to weaken this attachment. But after Matthew's visit home, his feelings on this subject seemed to have undergone a change. He never spoke unkindly of his native country, but he said decidedly that he preferred America. He probably found something in the manners of the people in England which made him feel more sensibly the distinctions of rank and station than he did here. He never said what had wrought the change in his feelings, but the change was decided, and as soon as he became of age he was naturalized in the legal form.

HIS EARLY FANCY FOR THE STAGE.

When Matthew was a child, in England, his "cleverness," as the English call it, his smartness or talent, as we should say, brought him early into notice. It was common at that time to have social gatherings, called Temperance Tea-Parties, where the price of admission was very low, and the amusement such as the guests could provide among themselves. Among the rest, little theatrical pieces, of their own contrivance, were very popular, and in these Matt was a useful performer. He was very little, but very bright, and he did for parts where a larger boy would not have answered. He spoke pieces, too, and tasted the pleasure of applause. This, perhaps, led him, when he was older, and had come to America, away from all his acquaintances, to take pleasure in attending the theatre; from which sprung the desire to become an actor. But it was no inferior station in the profession that he thought of. To be a Macready, a Forrest, or a Booth, *that* was the object of his ambition. Mr. B. by no means approved this idea, but he did not vigorously oppose it. He merely told Matthew the facts about the low standing of the theatrical profession in our day. Matthew, somewhat later, made

acquaintance with Mr. Gilbert and Mr. Barry, of
the Boston stage, and these gentlemen confirmed all
that Mr. B. had said, and decidedly discouraged
Matthew's devoting himself to the profession. He
gradually talked less about it, and as his mind expanded, and especially as he became interested in
his mechanical pursuits, he ceased ever to allude to
the stage as a profession for him.

It may seem strange that, with his early fondness
for scientific objects, he should have ever indulged
the thought of abandoning his occupation for another. But young people are not always consistent,
and Matthew, as an apprentice, saw only the least
attractive part of his calling. He had to make, over
and over again, the inferior parts of instruments,
never being intrusted with the higher portions,
which were the department of his employer himself.
But when Matthew became his own master, and
more, when he began to originate contrivances the
credit of which would be his own, he felt no disposition to abandon his art. He did not even contem-

plate ceasing to be a mathematical-instrument maker, when he should have acquired his collegiate education. He often spoke with enthusiasm of the advantage his handicraft trade would be to him in philosophical investigations. "Those who invented the telescope, the theodolite, and other instruments," he would say, "had to find workmen to carry out their ideas. If I have any thought of the kind, I can execute it myself." He estimated equally the benefit which he derived from his books. His friend, Dr. Bacon, had lent him Brewster's work on Optics and Dick's Practical Astronomer. These works delighted him, by giving him a reason for practices which he had already learned experimentally. In adapting the lens to the telescope, workmen usually ascertain by experiment the proper distance from the object-glass at which to place the lens. Matthew learned from his books how to calculate the focal distance of any lens, and consequently its proper position in the instrument. His ambition was to unite the characters of the skilful artificer and the accomplished scholar, — a character perhaps never yet exhibited to the world. There have been many mechanics who have acquired respectable literary cultivation, and there have been many learned men and statesmen who have been amateur mechanics; but Matthew's object was thoroughness in both departments.

MATTHEW'S RELIGIOUS OPINIONS.

When he was a boy, in England, there came to the place where he lived a party of surveyors, employed by government to make a survey of the whole of England. Among them were some Germans, who had accommodation in the house where Matthew lived. Matthew was often in their company, and heard them converse, sometimes, on religion. They had a light way of talking about matters usually held sacred, and infected Matthew somewhat with their notions; such as, that nothing is real but what we can see, touch, or otherwise subject to the examination of our senses; that religion is a matter of mystery; that it may be true, or may not be, and there is no demonstration on this side or on that. It was to counteract this way of thinking that Mr. B. lent him Paley's Natural Theology. This work argues for the existence of a Being, the intelligent cause of all things, possessing the attributes of wisdom, power, and goodness, and draws its proofs from the evident adaptation of the things we see around us to promote the happiness of living beings. If a traveller should find a watch lying upon the road, he would not hesitate to infer, from examining it, though he had never seen one before, that it was the work of some intelligent person, who had a design in making such an ingenious arrangement of wheels, springs, and pointers, all adapted to mark the lapse of time. The world, Paley contends, is such an instrument, or rather is full of such instruments, evidently designed for a purpose, and exhibiting the utmost ingenuity in contrivance to accomplish the purpose intended. This argument

Paley develops in a most interesting manner, carrying it through the various departments of the human frame, and then through other of the works of nature. Matthew found the argument satisfactory, and highly enjoyed Paley's treatment of it.

Still his mind would often revert to the supposed certainty of things which we see and handle, beyond that of those about which we merely reason. One day he met with a serious disappointment in his work. A part on which he had spent much careful labor was found imperfect in the finishing, and had to be done over again. The next Sunday he attended service at King's Chapel, and heard President Walker preach. He always enjoyed the President's discourses, for they stimulated the thinking faculty, which always gave him pleasure. On this occasion the preacher enforced his topic with his usual skill, and left his auditors, not only satisfied with the view he took, but wondering how anybody should ever have taken a different one. Matthew expressed his satisfaction in warm terms; yet, after

5

a pause, he added: "What the President says seems very true, but how do I know but that there may be another side to the question, and if I knew more I might see that he is mistaken? Now *there* is the difference between such matters and those in which I labor. Nothing whatever could prove to me that my circle is not a failure. I *see* it to be so, and there is no room for doubt." To this it was replied, that the evidence of the senses is but one kind of evidence, and not by any means the most trustworthy. He was reminded how deceptive that evidence is in regard to the movements of the heavenly bodies, and how many ages it took for men to learn, from a different kind of evidence, that it is the earth which turns round, and not the heavens. "Still," said he, "I am willing to believe my eyes and ears." This opened a wide conversation, which was but one of many that he had with his elder friend, in which the latter did what he could, without entering into argument, to give him correct notions of the higher subjects of knowledge, and teach him the office of faith.

"Faith," said Matthew, "is the evidence of things not seen," as if he meant to say that it was but equivalent to no evidence at all. "Not so," said his instructor. "You have faith in me, that I love you and mean to do you good; but you have no evidence but your inferences from what you observe in me." Matthew's thoughts on these subjects will be recognized as the natural growth of a mind of a mechanical turn. It is the opposite tendency to the "transcendental."

Here it would give his biographer great pleasure to be able to say that Matthew found in the pages of Scripture what science and observation fail to teach. To this point his elder friend endeavored to lead him, and flattered himself that, as time passed away, he made gradual approaches to it. But the engrossing nature of Matthew's pursuits (as is too generally the case with the young and ambitious) had prevented his paying much attention to sacred things; and, though there was no irreverence in his allusions to such subjects, there was not that concern for them which there ought to be in every thoughtful mind. His friend trusted to time, and to the silent influences which he might bring around him, to produce in him a religious character.

MATTHEW'S HABITS OF LIFE.

His habits of life were the natural result of his principles of self-tasking and self-devotion. To rise early; to bathe all over in cold water, without regard to the temperature of the weather; to dispense with an overcoat, till it was forced upon him by his more prudent friend; to study late at night, and in a room without a fire; — these are specimens of his way of life. He adopted a vegetable diet, because he could not reconcile it to his notions of right to slaughter animals for food. He declared that he relished his simple food, potatoes, rice, johnny-cakes, and particularly some nice porridge, which the lady at whose house he boarded cooked for him, better than he ever had done animal food. Against this notion his old-fashioned friend employed argument and joke, but without avail. He thought it would soon come to an end of itself, and therefore did not feel anxious about it; especially as, upon inquiring of some judicious medical friends upon the subject, he found them by no means strenuous in opposition to the practice, particularly in Matthew's case, whose temperament was decidedly ardent. So it went on, and, to all appearance, he throve well upon his simple fare, to which he adhered most scrupulously for the last eighteen months of his life. He was proud of the success of his experiment, and, finding that he kept up his flesh and strength, considered that he had demonstrated its good effects. One day he called at Mr. B.'s room at four o'clock in the afternoon. He came in with a countenance full of satisfaction, and told Mr. B. he had finished an instrument he was about, and had carried it home. He added, "I have not been in bed for thirty-two hours. I promised to have this job done this morning, but last evening it was not near done, and I have kept at it all night, and almost to this time; for I could not bear to have them call for it and find it unfinished. And now I don't feel at all tired; so you see what vegetable diet will do." Mr. B. felt really distressed, and replied, "Matthew, I do not praise you for this." He added earnest dissuasions from such lavish expenditure of health and life (for so he considered it), pointing to examples of individuals who had sacrificed both by similar imprudent conduct. Matthew replied, that he did not mean to do so again, but this was a special case; he had given his word, &c., &c.

The question will arise, to some minds, whether it was wise in Matthew's friend to encourage one so devoted to a special pursuit to add another to it, and that so arduous a one as the preparation for college. Mr. B. had this thought, and never stimulated Matthew in the slightest degree to get on with his studies. But he was also convinced, from his own experience, that the best sort of rest for mental exertion is found in change of occupation. The Latin exercise would banish the thoughts of the theodolite for a time from the mind, which mere inaction would fail to do. But as the crisis of the instrument approached, Matthew did in fact suspend his studies, and for a month or six weeks brought no lesson with him to the evening meeting, which was spent in reading or talk. They were reading the History of the French Revolution, finishing off with a chapter or two of Don Quixote; but, before and after the reading, there was time to talk over the progress of the instrument, and plans for the future.

CHAPTER IV.

THOUGH Matthew had been brought up in humble circumstances, and had been much in intercourse with the lowest classes, having crossed the ocean three times as a steerage passenger, an associate with the sailors and poor emigrants, he had contracted no taint of vulgarity. In all the intercourse which Mr. B. had with him, he never heard him utter a profane or indecent expression, and this, though he has stood by him at his work, when sometimes tools would not work well, or materials would slip or fall or otherwise prove refractory. Matthew told his friend many laughable stories of the scenes he had witnessed, but there was not one which might not have been told in the most refined circle of ladies and gentlemen, without the slightest impropriety. He often expressed, in general terms, his disgust at much that he had seen, but the details seem to have been rejected by his pure taste, so as to form no part of the stores of his memory.

He had one fault in conversation. As he felt strongly, he was apt to speak with energy disproportioned to the subject. One anecdote will illustrate this. In reading Macaulay's account of the trial of Warren Hastings they came to the passage where he speaks of the "silver voice" of Cowper, the clerk, who read the documents. "Silver voice," said Matthew, with a sneer, "what nonsense! I detest such phrases. They mean nothing." "I don't know," said Mr. B., coolly, "I think the phrase is not so bad. Perhaps he was thinking of the sound of a silver bell; at any rate, you may be sure Mr. Macaulay did not use the expression carelessly, and without reflection. And if he did, it is hardly worth while to get so excited about it.

You might say, 'I don't like it, I think it not a well-chosen expression;' but it is not necessary to *detest* it." They read on, and having finished their reading, drew round the fire. Mr. B. had quite forgotten the incident, when Matthew said, "I am afraid, sir, you don't tell me of my faults so much as I deserve. I was very foolish about that *silver voice*." "No, Matthew, not *very foolish*, only a little so, and I will promise to tell you all such faults as I see." The next meeting he was able to show Matthew a further proof that he had been too hasty in his criticism. The expression is in fact borrowed from a sonnet of the poet Cowper, addressed to his cousin Cowper, the clerk, alluding to this very occasion, and beginning, —

" Cowper, whose silver voice, tasked sometimes hard."

Matthew's vegetable diet often drew a sportive allusion. One day, sitting by the fire, eating an apple, he said, "Will you please lend me your knife to cut out this worm?" Mr. B. handed him the knife, and said, "As I know your prejudice against animal food, I will." "I have gone one step further, of late," said Matthew; "when I cut out a worm from an apple, I cut out a piece large enough to give him something to live on." Mr. B., smiling, rejoined, "But how can you justly take any part from him, as he had the first right?" "I have my rights too," said Matthew.

He was fond of quoting Shakespeare. Enjoying in prospect the success of his instrument, he would borrow the language of Stephano, in the Tempest, where he speaks of taking Caliban to England, to make a show of him, or sell him. "I will not take too much for him," he would say, with a knowing shake of the head, adding, "He shall pay for him that hath him, and that soundly."

But his favorite poet was Goldsmith. When any difficulty rose, he would say, —

" Every want that stimulates the breast
Becomes a source of pleasure when redressed;"

and, alluding to the case of those who have not had
the benefits of education, he would say, —

> "Unknown to them, when sensual pleasures cloy,
> To fill the languid pause with finer joy."

Another line, too, was often on his lips, —

> "To know the solid worth of self-applause."

Matthew's shop was in the fourth story of a
house on Washington Street, and in the corresponding story of the opposite house there was a room
occupied by seamstresses.   When Matthew lifted
his eyes from his work, he sometimes caught those
of his opposite neighbors, resting for a moment,
while the needle stood still in the hem.   A nod
and a smile sometimes followed, and kindly sympa-
thies darted across the street quicker than the spark
in Matthew's electrical machine.   One day he saw
an apple-woman, with her basket, dispensing her
wares among the girls.   Matthew was always fond
of an apple, so he beckoned to the woman to come
over to him.   Before long, she arrived with her

fruit, but would not allow him to buy any, presenting him with four of the finest as a present from his opposite neighbors. We may be sure this caused the nods and smiles to fly faster than ever from Matthew's side of the street. Next day he made a return for the civility by sending some fruit, the best he could get, to his fair friends.

Matthew was much amused, in reading the French Revolution, by a passage which describes the mechanical tastes of the king, Louis XVI. The historian says: "He never felt so happy as when, having dismissed his council, he could steal up the little staircase which led to his forge, which was situated in the roof of his palace, and where he found his fellow-laborer, a locksmith, named Gamin. The king was proud of showing his robust constitution by carrying about, with his own arms, the anvil and other tools with which he worked." Matthew laughed heartily at this. "I would n't have such a workman in *my* shop," said he.

We have not yet described his personal appearance. When Mr. B. first knew him, at about nineteen years old, he was rather small for his age. As he stood at his work-bench at Mr. Temple's, with coat off and sleeves rolled up, his appearance was that of a slender lad, about five feet in height. After that time he grew rapidly, and at his full growth was five feet nine inches tall, and weighed one hundred and thirty-five pounds. His hair was dark red, his complexion beautifully fair, his eyes blue, with light eyebrows and lashes, his nose well formed, his mouth somewhat large, with perfect teeth and bright red lips, and capable of a smile of the most winning expression. But the most striking feature of his face was his lofty forehead, surmounted with a pile of red hair, which he had not yet learned to arrange with skill. His cheeks were blooming, his step elastic, and his whole appearance that of vigorous health. His address was modest, yet self-possessed and prepossessing. If his eyebrows and eyelashes had been a shade darker, he would have been decidedly handsome.

He always dressed neatly, and was very cleanly in his habits. Mr. B. thought that he observed an exception to this in the state of his nails, and spoke to him about it. But he found that the discoloration was the necessary consequence of his work, and that it was not to be washed off. Matthew proudly added, "Though my nails look black, I will not yield to any of the young men you meet in society in cleanliness."

Matthew found many difficulties in making his instrument. There were parts of it which as an apprentice he had never made; nor had he ever seen them made, for it is not allowed to an apprentice to quit his work to look over his master or older workmen to see their processes. In making such parts he had to learn his business by doing it. It is therefore no wonder if he made some mistakes. When these happened, he usually took courage and tried again; and generally succeeded in a second attempt. One day he met with a failure so serious that he could not at once pluck up heart to begin again. He went home to dinner, and after dinner, instead of hastening back to the shop as usual, he sat on the sofa, with his head on his hand, every now and then uttering a word or two to himself, expressive of his mortification and disappointment. At last he started up and spoke to the landlady's eldest son, a boy of about twelve. " Henry, have not you got something to amuse us ? Go get some of your playthings." Henry brought his magic lantern, an old toy which had long ago lost its attraction. Matthew took it, and with the children for an audience, began to exhibit its wonders. His spirits revived, he was a boy again ; and so droll, so diverting in his part of showman, that he kept the circle in a roar of laughter, forgot his griefs, and enjoyed the fun as much as any of them. Next morning he returned to his work with renewed vigor.

It was while he was in one of his most serious perplexities that an opportunity occurred of doing a kind office. Bridget, the Irish girl in Mr. S.'s kitchen, had sent home money to pay her sister's passage to Boston; but Susan had taken passage to New York, and Bridget was in great distress, thinking that her sister would arrive in a strange city, destitute of money to carry her the rest of the way. Bridget did not know any one in New York to ask to receive her sister and help her on her way; she only knew that the name of the ship was the Dreadnaught. Matthew asked advice of his friend Mr. B., who undertook to inquire among his commercial friends, and learn the address of the owners of the ship. The next time he saw Matthew, which was after an interval of three days, he gave him the information; but Matthew had already learned it, written to the gentlemen, and got their answer promising to see Susan on her arrival, and deliver to her any money that might be sent for her use. All worked well. Susan arrived safe in Boston, and both sisters felt deeply obliged to Matthew for his help in their embarrassment.

Matthew did not allow his cares and occupations

to make him forgetful of his friends in England, but kept up an active correspondence with his excellent parents and other connections. He often alluded tenderly to his parents, and expressed the wish to do something to promote their comfort. "My mother is old," he would say, "and it is too hard for her to do all the housework. I want to be able to send her enough to hire a girl to help her." As his instrument approached completion, and he expected soon to receive two hundred and fifty dollars for it (having already received fifty), he consulted his friend as to the advisableness of sending one hundred dollars to his parents. His adviser doubted whether it would be judicious to take so much from his business at that time, but if Matthew had lived to receive his pay, a part of it would surely have found its way across the Atlantic.

For one of his improvements he claimed a patent, which has since been granted. "My plan is," he said, " to sell my patent for enough to carry me through college." But he did not mean to give up his shop while pursuing his college course. On the contrary, it was his intention to work at his trade in the vacations, and at intervals of leisure. "I have other thoughts in my head," said he. "I cannot but .think that the telescope is capable of being much improved." He went on to state some of his views upon this subject, but his biographer does not remember .his remarks sufficiently to report them.

CHAPTER V.

MATTHEW'S REMOVAL TO CAMBRIDGE.

ONE of Matthew's improvements on the theodolite related to the part on which the figures and markings are inscribed, which figuring and marking is called the *graduation*. His improvement consisted in inscribing the graduation in white lines on a black ground. It is usually inscribed in black lines on a white ground. His reasons for preferring his method are given in a paper, appended to this memoir, which paper was drawn up by himself, unaided, and is here presented without alteration, except in the spelling of a word or two. His idea, when he wrote it, was that his method might be applied to book-printing, as it has already been to the printing of diagrams in works of science.

This idea was, perhaps, chimerical; but that does not detract from the correctness of his reasoning, nor from the desirableness of his method for such purposes as those of his instrument.

Matthew's method of inscribing his white graduations was this. After the graduations were engraved or impressed on the brass, he immersed the part in a solution of silver, and by the action of the galvanic battery caused the silver to be deposited on the brass, filling up the graduations, and covering all the rest of the surface with a coating of silver. Then, with his file or his turning tool, he removed the superfluous silver, leaving the white metal in the engraved lines. Thus far he had used a well-known process, called electrotyping. The next step was to put a black color on the brass surface, so as to show the white letters to advantage. The difficulty here was to blacken the brass intensely, without discoloring the silver at all. Matthew could nowhere find any directions how to do this. His scientific friends, even, thought it

could not be done. Matthew set himself vigorously
to experimenting. When recovering from sickness
he had read the Conversations on Chemistry, which
had given him the groundwork of the science, and
enabled him to understand and apply the directions
given in more practical works. He soon learned
how to prepare his solutions, and to impart a
bronze dye to his brass, but for a long while he
could contrive no method of doing this without
at the same time discoloring the silver marks. But
he persevered; day after day he spent in experimenting; solutions were made and tried, only to
be rejected and thrown away. Every experiment
cost both money and time; the materials of his solutions were to be bought, and when the solution was
made, the metal pieces had to be submitted to it
for hours, before the effect could be judged of. It
was a discouraging process; but at last a lucky
thought struck him. Perhaps he might hasten the
operation by applying his galvanic battery. The
effect was admirable. The bronzing which had be-

fore taken hours to accomplish was done in as many minutes. Aided by this discovery, he made rapid progress in experimenting. He soon selected the solution which would impart the best and darkest bronze; and found, to his delight, that, whatever the cause might be, the color, so laid on, did not affect the silver lettering in the slightest degree. For this discovery Matthew has since obtained a patent.

It was at this stage of his progress that he became acquainted with the gentlemen at Cambridge. He tried his "leucographic graduation" on a thermometer scale. "Leucographic" means, *written in white*, from two Greek words. He took his thermometer to Cambridge Observatory, and exhibited it to Professor Bond. That gentleman, in a note to the writer, says, "His leucographic graduation impressed me very favorably. White divisions inlaid upon a dark ground would have many advantages over the customary method of exhibiting the graduations of astronomical instruments." Appre-

ciating Matthew's improvement so highly, it may
easily be imagined that Professor Bond's reception
of him was very gratifying to him. From the
Observatory, Matthew went next to call upon Professor Eustis, of the Scientific School. He found
that gentleman engaged at dinner. Matthew sent
in his card and was going away, but the Professor
no sooner read the name than he started from the
table, ran out into the entry, calling, "Mr. Edwards!
Mr. Edwards! pray don't go; I am very glad to
see you." He had heard of Matthew's improvements through some of the young men of the Scientific School, more than one of whom had been
frequent visitors at Matthew's shop, and felt a warm
interest in his operations. Professor Eustis looked
at the thermometer, and heard Matthew's account
of his other improvements, and took him up stairs
to show him some specimens of work that he had
lately received from Europe He would have had
Matthew stay to dinner, but Matthew's "dinner of
herbs" was already over. He next called on Pro-

fessor Lovering, who received him in the same cordial manner, discussing with him his new contrivances with the manner, not of a teacher to a pupil, but of one man of science with another.

Matthew came home delighted with the reception he had met with. His object in going to Cambridge was partly to look out for accommodations there for his workshop and home. He had made up his mind that Cambridge would be as favorable a place for his business as Washington Street in Boston, and certainly a much more pleasant one. He could not expect transient jobs there, but he did not desire them. He had made arrangements for making six more instruments of the same kind as the one he was now employed on, and by carrying on six at a time, great saving in time and expense would be made. "When I get the first one done," he used to say, "with my patterns all made, and all my processes perfected, you will see how fast I will turn them off."

He found accommodations in Cambridge which

7

suited him exactly. He could get twice as much room, with better light and better access, for two thirds as much money as he had been paying. He arranged to remove his establishment there, and take possession the 1st of January. He enjoyed the prospect with enthusiasm. "Here," said he, "at this window I shall have my bench; just see, right opposite that apple-tree; I shall have the birds singing there while I am at my work." At the adjoining house, where he was to take his meals, there was a garden. He stipulated for leave to work in it as much as he chose. He had learned something about such work when he was in the country, and he enjoyed the prospect of turning his information to account. There were to be some students of the College among his fellow-boarders. Matthew did not fail to think of the subject of dress, in this connection. He had him an apron made to come up close under his chin, so as to protect his shirt-bosom, and with sleeves to come down over his shirt-sleeves when rolled up, and button round the arm above the elbow. Thus when meal-time came he might throw off his apron, and be at once in neat and clean attire to go in and sit at table with the young gentlemen. To prevent the noise of his anvil from disturbing the students, who were to occupy the rooms under him, he was going to have a carpet on his floor. He flattered himself his shop would look so neat that he should not be ashamed to have ladies come to see him; and several had promised to look in and see him, when he got established.

Thus were things situated when the last week of 1859 arrived. On Sunday, which was Christmas-day, Matthew was at his brother's house, apparently well, and certainly in high spirits. He read to his brother and sister an amusing story in a magazine, and laughed in his usual hearty way at it. They have a window looking up the street, and they followed him with their eyes as he went away, while he occasionally turned round and exchanged nods with them. On Monday he was at his shop half the day, but feeling some rheumatic pains in his limbs, did not return to his work after dinner. In the night he suffered much pain, so that next morning he got one of his fellow-boarders to call at Mr. B.'s door, and desire him to come and see him. Mr. B. went immediately, and found Matthew suffering pains of the same sort as those which had afflicted him two years ago. Dr. Coolidge, who attended him then, was sent for, and prescribed for him. He suffered a good deal through the day, but had intermissions, during which he could enjoy his book. Dr. Coolidge lent him the life of Franklin. From certain points of similarity in his history to that of Franklin, his friend, Mr. B., had early procured for him the life of that great man. But the penurious maxims of Poor Richard were by no means pleasing to Matthew, and the book was laid aside. He now took it up again, and in the course of Tuesday and Wednesday made good progress in it. But it did not give him a very exalted impression of Franklin's character. One incident in particular he remarked upon. It seems Franklin, when a young printer, in London, boarded with a widow lady, who was kind to him, and being herself an intelligent person, enjoyed his society, and was an agreeable companion to him. In spite of this, when Franklin found that he could save one and sixpence a week by changing his boarding-house, he did not scruple to do it, and would have done it, but for his landlady's consenting to abate as much or more from her price, which she did, rather than part with him. On the strength of this incident Matthew was ready to dethrone Franklin from his position of a great man. He had to be told that Franklin's greatness consisted rather in his intellectual than in his moral qualities, and that nobody ever set him up as a model of generosity.

Matthew was apt to fall into a line of remark very peculiar for a young man of apparently vigorous health and of good prospects. "I do not see why one should dread death," he would say. "For my part, I have no preference to live rather than

7 *

die." As they sat together on the sofa, Wednesday afternoon, Matthew spoke in this way. Mr. B. tried to give him a different view of things. He reminded him of the pleasures in store for him as he grew older, in visiting Europe, and seeing those places famous in history of which he had read; Matthew admitted it all, but still repeated his entire indifference, whether to live or die. Mr. B. left him, with a kind parting, but by no means a desponding one, for he saw no reason for more apprehension than usual.

Matthew had found lying in bed so painful, on Tuesday night, that he dreaded to encounter another such. His kind landlady fixed up a sofa-bed for him in the sitting-room, where warmth was kept up all night, and the Doctor gave him some opiates, which enabled him to sleep. The lady of the house occupied an adjoining room to him, and looked in twice in the course of the night, and both times found him sleeping as calmly as an infant. He rose early, and as his young fellow-boarders came down, and inquired how he was, he replied, "As well as I could expect." Things looked rather favorable, and his landlady was pursuing her usual occupations in the room with him, when she heard a gasp, as she expressed it, and looking round, saw his head fall back. She ran to him, calling to those in the next room to bring water, for she thought he had fainted. Water was brought, and she threw some in his face, and laid him down on the sofa. One of the boarders brought hartshorn and applied it to his nose. He turned away, and that was the last sign of voluntary motion.

Just then, at about nine o'clock, Mr. B. arrived. He saw him lifeless, surrounded by the weeping women of the house, and by the young men boarders, all in great distress, for he was a general favorite. The shock to this friend, who for nearly three years had been so intimately connected with Matthew, had shared all his hopes, and rejoiced in every new development of his powers, was overwhelming. Yet he knew too well the nature of the complaint to feel surprised at the event. He stooped down and kissed him, and then, having sent one of the young men to communicate the sad news to the elder brother, departed.

The funeral took place on Saturday, December 31, at King's Chapel. There was an attendance unusually large for the obsequies of one so young, and unconnected with society by family ties. Among those present were some of the most distinguished individuals of our city for station and merit. The coffin was almost covered with flowers, the gift of friends whom Matthew's own merits had won for him. The body was carried to Mount Auburn Cemetery, and deposited in the lot of his friend Mr. B.

In reviewing the fate of one so worthy of living, and so early taken away, we are apt to ask ourselves whether it might not have been prevented if he had been less ambitious, less self-exacting. The reply is, if he had been so, he would not have been himself, but another. Those qualities constituted his individuality; and though we may regret that he had not with them more prudence, it is like our regret that he had not a better physical constitution. His peculiarities both of mind and body were God's gift; and it is our part to be grateful for what he gave, and not to repine at what he was pleased to withhold.

So passed away this energetic, pure, and loving spirit. Among the last of his poetical readings were those lines of Milton in which he laments a young friend snatched away by a similar premature death; and surely to no one could they be more fitly applied than to the subject of our memoir.

"Fame is the spur that the pure spirit doth raise,
  (That last infirmity of noble mind,)
To scorn delights, and live laborious days;
  But the fair guerdon when we hope to find,
And think to burst out into sudden blaze,
  Comes the blind Fury with the abhorred shears,
And clips the thin-spun life. But not the praise. . . . . .
  That lives and spreads aloft by the pure eyes,
And perfect witness of all-judging Jove.
As he pronounces lastly on each deed,
Of so much fame in Heaven expect thy meed."

APPENDIX.

No. I.

INDENTURE OF APPRENTICESHIP.

WE here give a copy of Matthew's indenture of apprenticeship. It is written on parchment, and bears on the corner a stamp, marked *one pound*. The document is *indented*, that is, cut in dents or scallops on the edge, from whence comes the name.

"This indenture witnesseth that Matthew Edwards, of Derby, in the County of Derby, by and with the consent of his father, William Edwards, of the same place, doth put himself apprentice to John Davis, of Derby, aforesaid, Optician, to learn his art, and with him, after the manner of an apprentice, to serve, from the day of the date of these presents, until the thirteenth day of July, in the year of our Lord, one thousand eight hundred and fifty-nine, during which term the said Apprentice his said Master faithfully shall serve, his secrets keep, his lawful commands everywhere gladly do. He shall do no damage to his said Master, nor see it done by others, but to his power shall let, or forthwith give warning to his said Master, of the same. He shall not waste the goods of his said Master, nor give or lend them unlawfully to any; he shall neither buy nor sell without his said Master's leave; Taverns, Inns, or Alehouses he shall not haunt; at Cards, Dice, Tables, or any other unlawful games he shall not play; Matrimony he shall not contract; nor from the service of his said Master, by day, absent himself; but in all things, as a faithful Apprentice, he shall behave himself towards his said Master and all his family during the said term.

" And the said John Davis, the said Apprentice in the Art of an Optician, which he now useth, shall and will teach and instruct, or cause to be taught and instructed, in the best way and manner that he can, and shall pay unto the said Apprentice, during the first year of the said term the sum of two shillings

and sixpence per week; during the second year
thereof the sum of three shillings and sixpence per
week; during the third year the sum of four shillings
and sixpence per week; during the fourth year the
sum of five shillings and sixpence per week; during
the fifth year the sum of six shillings and sixpence
per week; during the sixth year the sum of seven
shillings and sixpence per week; during the seventh
year the sum of eight shillings and sixpence per
week; during the eighth year the sum of nine shillings and sixpence per week; and during the remain-
der of the said term the sum of ten shillings and
sixpence per week.

"And for the true performance of all and every,
the said Covenants and Agreements, each of the said
Parties bindeth himself unto the other firmly ·by
these presents. In witness whereof the Parties
aforesaid to these Indentures have hereunto respec-
tively set their Hands and Seals, the Fourth day of
March, in the fourteenth year of the Reign of our
Sovereign Lady, Victoria, by the Grace of God, of
the United Kingdom of Great Britain and Ireland,
Queen, Defender of the Faith; and in the year of

our Lord, one thousand eight hundred and fifty-one.

" Sealed and delivered (being first duly stamped) in the presence of
    I. H. PICKERING,
      Solicitor, Derby."

The signatures have been cut away, and across the face of the Indenture the following words are written:—

" We the undersigned cancel this Indenture.

"Derby, March 7, 1853.

       " (Signed,) MATTHEW EDWARDS,

            WILLIAM EDWARDS,

            JOHN DAVIS."

And on the back there is written:—

" Matthew Edwards has been in my employ for two years, during which time I have found him uniformly honest, and this indenture was cancelled by mutual consent.

        " JOHN DAVIS, *Optician.*

"Derby, March 7, 1853."

No. II.

EXTRACTS FROM CORRESPONDENCE.

To Mr. B.

Barrington, N. H., July 23, 1858.

THIS is a cloudy day, so that we cannot work on the hay, and it affords me a good opportunity of writing to you. Perhaps more particulars about the place I am now staying at would be interesting. The house has a most pleasant situation, on a hill which overlooks the road, called "Green Hill." In the front of the house there are several beautiful shade-trees, and I think it is the most neatly built and finished farm-house I have seen in the neighborhood. The farm consists of about one hundred and fifty acres, all of which is in a very good state of cultivation. The farmer's wife is one of the kindest women I have ever met with.

To THE SAME.

Barrington, August 8, 1858.

I am writing this letter in a great hurry, although it is Sunday; for we have to work on the hay to-day, as it is a very good hay-day, and we have some quantity out, which we want to get in before night.

I am glad you called my attention to the observation of the natural objects which surround me. I think I have a natural disposition to observe these things; but your remarks on the subject will cause me to pay more attention to them than I should otherwise do. My stay in the country has enabled me to appreciate those little courtesies which we offer to one another in polite society, and which I was too apt to consider as affectation; for here I see an almost total suspension of them, and the result is a perpetual wrangling; which is produced by their disregard for each other's feelings, and their licentious use of language; which would be inadmissible in polite society.

I have got the books you sent, and thank you for them. I hope you keep a strict account of all the money you expend for me, as I desired you to do.

I regret to think that I have nothing more to offer you in return for all your favors, but my unprofitable affection; but I flatter myself by thinking *that* will be acceptable, and remain yours ever affectionately.

The following are of a later date by a year. In 1859 he took a vacation of a few weeks, and paid a visit to his friends at Barrington.

To the Same.

Barrington, July 20, 1859.

DEAR PATER, — I did not get yours of the 15th until yesterday, when I took a ride on horseback to Dover. Since I have arrived in the country I have enjoyed myself very much, and I already begin to feel the benefit of it. It would be scarcely more of a task for you to imagine what I have been doing than for me to tell you. I have had but one horseback ride; but one drive with the farmer's daughter; mowed once; have walked but little with my female friends; have been in search neither of flowers nor minerals; have not read more than three or four hours during the week. So much for the negative side of the question. All I can say on the positive side is, that I have generally and uniformly enjoyed myself.

I have read both the poems you pointed out to me, but do not think them at all equal to Goldsmith. I think the Elegy (Gray's Elegy, written in a Country Churchyard) is superior to the Ode (Ode on the distant prospect of Eton College). There does not seem to me to be anything very definite or applicable in Gray's Ode on Eton College; and the impres-

8 *

sion left on my mind after reading it is something like that experienced after hearing one of R. W. Emerson's Lectures.

You ask me for my opinion on Gray's alliteration. I do not think my poetical taste sufficiently developed and critical to give an *opinion* on such a matter; but as you desire it, I will give you my *impression.* To my ear it seems to have no bad effect on the rhythm of verse. I think the effect is especially pleasing and appropriate in the line you cite, —

"Ruin seize thee, ruthless king!"

In this instance it seems to increase the earnestness of the expression, and render it more emphatic. But there is one argument which I think should condemn its general adoption, and restrain other poets from imitating Gray in this particular; that is, it is an additional shackle to expression, and restricts the poet's choice of words to a still narrower range. The rhyme and rhythm of verse are to the poet what the use of the chisel is to the sculptor, merely the mechanical part. It is the sublimity and truthfulness of his conception which prove the poet and the man of genius.

I am now in the woods, scribbling off with a lead pencil, intending to copy it in the house. I cannot say that I am alone, for at this moment I am surrounded by thirty or forty most vigilant and musical mosquitoes, whose repeated attacks by no means increase the pleasures of my situation.

To a Friend in England.

Boston, February 8, 1858.

I have many ambitious designs, which are dearer to me than life; for without the hope of accomplishing them, life would be to me insignificant and worthless. But my principal design is to get a thorough education, for on the achievement of this one depends the success of the rest. The getting this thorough education will occupy at least the next eight years of my life.

. . . . . .

There have been moments when visions of future domestic happiness presented themselves vividly to my imagination, — domestic happiness which I fear will never be to me anything more substantial than a vision. My imagination in a moment carried me

through a brilliant and successful period of active
life, until it brought me to that period when the
mind turns from the active scenes of life, and seeks
retirement and repose, that it may enjoy the mental
harvest it has gathered. Then I saw myself in a
cottage, far from the bustle and din of city life; — a
lawn resplendent with verdure spread out before me;
the wild rose-bush and sweet-brier surrounded the
door of my cottage, perfuming the air with their
sweet odors; the birds sung on the trees; a rivulet
sparkled in the distance; and by my side stood the
partner of my life, — a woman possessed of a noble
and cultivated mind; one who had accompanied me
through many winding paths, sharing my joys and
sorrows, my successes and disappointments.

This was a happy state; but it was only a dream.
In those dreams I forgot my cold attic in Boston; I
forgot the rigid economy I should have to practice,
and the difficulties I should have to encounter, before
I could start in life with the education and accom-
plishments I desire.

To the Same..

Boston, December 18, 1859.

To speak candidly, I do not think I have the right sort of mind to make any woman happy. I am too much in love with the sublime mysteries of nature to have much love left for a wife. I would sacrifice every other pleasure on earth to know what power it is in nature that animates matter; or to know why some men are born with noble dispositions, and others with dispositions quite the opposite. I would devote my life to a labor which should promise to yield up to man another sublime truth in the science of Astronomy, or in any way assist in the conquest of mind over matter.

To Dr. Rush.

· [Dr. Rush, hearing from him his intention of going to England, was impressed with the idea that this interruption of his plan of study proved a want of stability and perseverance. He wrote to him strongly on this point, and the following are extracts from Matthew's letter in reply.]

Boston, November 8, 1857.

When I started for Philadelphia, my plan was to
work at my trade until I had completed my apprenticeship, and then, after a little preparation, to go on
the stage. You recommended me to get a knowledge of the languages, and to study mathematics, and
the other elementary branches of education. Now,
since I left Philadelphia I have steadily devoted all
my evenings to these studies, and I intend to con-
tinue to do so for the next three or four years of
my life.

It seems to me there are a great many things in
nature yet unanalyzed, and which require the same
kind of philosophical reasoning that you have
brought to bear on the subject of the voice. Now
I should like to have the pleasure (if I have the
ability) of carrying on this kind of philosophical
analysis, — this analysis which finds out the truth of
things; but before an individual can add to the stock
of knowledge, he has first to learn what is already
known; and if I have to gain my knowledge and
education by studying a few hours every evening,
after working hard all day, I shall not only have to
sacrifice every social and domestic comfort of life,

but I shall find myself an old man and ready to die before I am in possession of the materials to think with.

In considering these things, I hope you will not charge me with unsteadiness if in three or four years from now I should inform you that I have left my trade, at least for a time, and am devoting my whole time to the improvement of my education.

.I admit that my going home retarded the progress of my studies, but I think on this point you may excuse me; for it is to be expected that a boy leaving home before he was fifteen years old should have a desire to see his parents after an absence from them of more than four years; and I considered it a duty which I owed to those who had provided for and protected me during the most helpless part of my life.

Your letter is far more valuable to me than one of commendation, for it reminds me of my weak points, and encourages me to conquer them; and it has a tendency to allay that feeling of pride and self-conceit which is too apt to creep over the mind of aspiring youth.

In your letter you speak of the short time left to

you, and of uncompleted designs. Let me assure you that I would not trespass for a moment upon this most valuable time; and I could not wish you to devote to an individual that which is of value to mankind. You have already done more for me than my wildest imagination could have led me to expect, and I ask no more.

Hoping this will find you recovered from your late indisposition, I have the honor to remain your greatly indebted and devoted humble friend, &c.

No. III.

A PROPOSED CHANGE IN THE METHOD OF PRINTING.

To the Editor of the ——— ———.

Sir: — In recently pursuing a course of studies on Optics, it occurred to me that an important improvement might be made in the present mode of printing, which I feel an irresistible desire to communicate to you, and (if you think my thoughts on this subject worthy the honor) through your columns to the public. The idea I have to offer has, no doubt, risen in the minds of many besides myself, therefore all the claim I can make to originality is simply to say that I never saw it in print, or heard it expressed by any individual.

My idea is briefly this:—We may improve the present mode of printing by reversing it; instead of printing black letters on a white ground, print white letters on a black ground. As it may not be at once apparent why this should constitute an improvement, I will attempt an explanation.

My argument is based on the principles of light and vision, as expounded by optical writers. These gentlemen tell us that white light (as emitted from the sun) is composed of seven different colors; and they account for the different colors possessed by the various objects which surround us, on the principle that these objects have the property of absorbing some of the colors of light, and reflecting others. For example, an object which appears to us red, absorbs all the colors but red, and *that* it reflects into the eye, giving it the peculiar appearance we denominate *red*.

Following out this principle, white and black can-

9   G

not be considered as colors, since an object which appears *white* has the property of reflecting (and absorbing) all the colors equally, so that light falling on such an object is not decomposed into its different colors; consequently no color is produced; and an object appearing *black* has the property of absorbing all the light which falls upon it. These principles being admitted, let us apply them to our present subject. When we look on a printed sheet of paper, how do we see the letters? It will be answered, "By the contrast produced by black and white." But let us examine this a step further, and see how these two qualities produce their effect upon the eye. According to the acknowledged principles of optical science, the black part of the printed paper absorbs all the light which falls upon it; hence it follows that the white part of the paper is the only part which reflects light into the eye, and produces what may be called a positive impression on the retina. Now the letters produce their effect in a different and opposite manner, which may be called a negative impression; that is to say, they are made evident to our visual faculties by their property of absorbing the light, and thus interrupting the uniform impression which would otherwise be made by the white paper. Let us now look at the page of a printed book or newspaper, and notice the relative proportions of space occupied by the letters and blank paper. In the majority of cases we find the white portions of the page, taken collectively, to occupy a space about double the size of the black portions. From a view of these facts it appears that in reading one page of a book the eye is taxed as much as it would be in reading two pages, if the letters were white on a black ground.

Persons who have not very strong eyes are often heard to complain of a confusion or *blur* they experience, after having read a short time. I think if the proposed improvement were adopted, it would have a tendency to alleviate in some degree this evil, which is no doubt caused by the retina's incapacity to bear a strong and continued impression of light; consequently the parts exposed to the action of light become irritated or inflamed; this inflammation spreads, thus having the effect to obscure the letters by equalizing the sensation over the whole retina. If our theory is correct, it is easy to understand how such individuals might receive benefit from the proposed improvement. In the first place, it would enable us to read by subjecting a much less portion of the retina to the action of light, and thus proportionably retard the approach of inflammation; secondly, when the retina became inflamed, the effect would have farther to spread before obscuring the letters. Besides these benefits, there is every reason to suppose that the letters would make a more forcible and definite impression on the eye; and thus materially aid the precision of reading. When we read, our object is to see the printed characters, not the paper; then, why not let them make the impression on the eye? In the present mode of printing, the mind is constrained to take cognizance of things omitted, which is always more of a task than to examine that which is brought boldly before its notice.

Having, perhaps, already occupied too much of your time, or taken up too much space in your columns, I submit my thoughts to your candid criticism, and to that of your intelligent readers.

OCULUS.

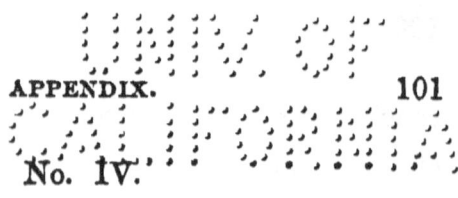

No. IV.

NOTE FROM PROFESSOR G. P. BOND.

Observatory of Harvard College,
Cambridge, January 9, 1860.

DEAR SIR:—In replying to your inquiries respecting Mr. Edwards, I would desire to be understood as expressing my impressions, gathered from two or three interviews, rather than a competent estimate of his abilities as an artist, which my limited acquaintance with him would scarcely enable me to form.

On the few occasions of our meeting, he seemed to be quite carried away with an enthusiastic desire to introduce novel principles and improvements into the construction of instruments, and, as was to be expected in one so young, he showed some want of familiarity with the actual state of the art. A larger experience would have tended to restrain his zeal. Still we must rememder that much is often accomplished by venturing further upon untried ground than prudence would dictate,—new principles and ideas must have their advocates, if they are ever to get a foothold.

There is one of Mr. Edwards's proposed improvements which impressed me very favorably, and which it must be a source of deep regret to all his friends that he did not live to perfect. I mean that which he termed the "leucographic" graduation. White divisions inlaid upon a dark ground would have many advantages over the customary method of exhibiting the graduations of astronomical instruments.

When I last saw him he was full of confidence in his plan, and I confess that it had my strongest sympathy and encouragement, although I was, of course, not a competent judge of the practicability of the mechanical means by which he proposed to accomplish it. Looking only at the end proposed, I should not hesitate to characterize it as one of capital importance, and well deserving all the attention which Mr. Edwards had devoted to it.

Respectfully yours,

G. P. BOND.

NOTE. — Matthew perfected his method of leucographic graduation after his interview with Professor Bond. He made out a specification of his processes, and forwarded it to Washington, with his claim for a patent, which was granted. He also prepared a thermometer scale, with leucographic graduations, which exhibits his design carried into execution.

No. V.

FROM PROFESSOR WILLIAM B. ROGERS, OF THE UNIVERSITY OF VIRGINIA.

Boston, February 5, 1860.

MY DEAR SIR:—The process of "leucographic graduation," invented by our young friend, Matthew Edwards, and for which he obtained a patent, a short time before his death, has always struck me as an improvement of great practical importance.

The advantage of silver lines on a nearly black ground is a necessary result of those optical laws which our young friend so well understood and explained; and would be conceded, perhaps, without experimental proof. Yet on inspecting a thermometer-scale prepared by this process, persons, even the most experienced in graduated instruments, would, I think, be *surprised* at the extent to which such a scale excels in *distinctness* the clearest graduations in general use.

The process by which this valuable result is attained is so simple, inexpensive, and certain, and its applications are so numerous and obviously advantageous, that I think it deserves to be strongly commended to all who are interested in the branch of art to which it appertains.

Yours, very truly,

WILLIAM B. ROGERS.

No. VI.

FROM PROFESSOR H. L. EUSTIS.

Cambridge, Mass., April 2, 1860.

MY DEAR SIR : — Your account of Edward's visit to me is entirely correct. He brought with him a specimen of his leucographic scales, and we had some conversation about the possibility of protecting them from oxidation. If this can be done, they certainly possess decided advantages over the old scales. The difficulty of reading a finely graduated vernier on account of the reflections becomes very fatiguing to the eye. His theodolite I did not see, but one of my pupils made a drawing of the levelling apparatus, which was one of the novelties introduced in it. This appeared to me to be an improvement upon the old method.

Yours truly,

H. L. EUSTIS.

No. VI.

DESCRIPTION OF THE LEVELLING APPARATUS OF EDWARDS'S IMPROVED THEODOLITE.

We are indebted to Mr. Edward L. Adams, of the Lawrence Scientific School, for the accompanying figures of the Levelling Apparatus invented by Mr. Edwards, and for the following description.

Figure 1 represents a vertical section of the levelling adjustments of the common theodolite. Figure 2 represents the levelling adjustments of Edwards's improved theodolite. In Fig. 1, $Q\,Q$ is the lower stationary plate, fastened to the tripod by means of the screw $S\,S$. It bears the weight of the instrument by means of the levelling screws K, L, which pass through the plate $P\,P$, to which is attached the spherical ball B, which is held firmly against the jaws J, J, of the lower plate, and thus prevents the upper plate from being removed too far from the lower one, while at the same time it allows a rotary motion in the upper plate. The lower graduated

circle (not shown in the figure) is attached to the spindle A, which moves within the ball B.

In Figure 2, $Q\,Q$ represents the lower portion of the instrument, bearing arms R, R, and fastened to the tripod by the screw $S\,S$. It has jaws $J\,J$ against which moves the spherical ball B, which is attached to the upper plate $P\,P$, by means of the screw $T\,T$. The ball is held in place by the accurately fitted ring E, which is screwed to the lower portion of the instrument. The arms $R\,R$ are stiffened at their extremities by a horizontal ring (not shown in the figure). The levelling screws $K\,L$ pass through the arms $F\,F$ of the upper plate $P\,P$. The axes of the screws are perpendicular to these arms, and also to the extended radius of the ball B, which radius makes an angle of 37° with the vertical line passing through the centre of the instrument, and passes through the arms $F\,F$. The lower end of the levelling screw moves upon a curve formed upon the upper face of the arm R, which curve is so constructed that the axis of the screw is always normal to it. The upper horizontal circle, which carries the compass, is connected with the tapering spindle A, which turns within the spindle D which is connected with the lower graduated circle, neither of which circles are shown in the figure. The spindle D turns within the ball B.

There are several manifest improvements in Edwards's levelling apparatus, over that in common use. First, the levelling screws are used only to adjust the upper plates when out of level, the weight of the instrument being borne by the ring E, while, in the common instrument, the weight is borne by the screws only, thus causing friction that wears out the threads. Secondly, owing to the thickness of the jaws in Fig. 2, as compared with those in Fig. 1, the friction caused by their contact with the ball is distributed over a larger surface, thus causing less wear between them, and better preserving the sphericity of the ball than in Fig. 1, in which the jaws are made very thin, and have a tendency to wear upon the ball, and wear away themselves, owing to the concentration of the friction between the ball and jaws to a narrow ring, which the surface of the jaws presents to the ball. This friction soon increases the diameter of the jaws to equal that of the ball, in which case it is crowded through the jaws, and the instrument is useless until repaired.

Thirdly, the screws in Fig. 2 always work to the best advantage, their axes being constantly normal to the surfaces against which they press, whereas in Fig. 1 the upper ends only have a constantly normal pressure, and the lower ends of the axes are normal to the surface of the lower plate, against which they press, only when the two plates are exactly parallel.

ADVERTISEMENT.

THE mechanical inventions of the late Matthew Edwards are offered for sale.

They consist, first, of an improved method of *bronzing* or darkening the surfaces of metals, applicable in particular to the graduating of mathematical instruments, in the manner called by the inventor " leucographic graduation, or the production of white lines on a dark ground." This process is secured by patent.

Secondly, of an improved method of levelling or adjusting, horizontally, mathematical instruments. This improvement removes the imperfection found in instruments as usually constructed, viz. that the levelling screws work hard, and are apt to get out of order.

A complete set of patterns for the construction of a Theodolite upon this system is to be sold, together with the right to employ this method.

Apply to EZRA LINCOLN, Civil Engineer, No. 4 Court Street, or to ENOCH EDWARDS, Executor, East Canton Street, Boston.

WALKER, WISE, & CO.'S
NEW JUVENILE BOOKS.

All the Children's Library.

This *entirely new and original series* of Juveniles combines several especially attractive features. The plan adopted is that of *gradation*, the first two books on the list being designed for very young children, just commencing to read. Numbers 3 and 4 meet the requirements of those three or four years older; while the last two of the set will interest older boys and girls, and may be read with pleasure by almost any one.

6 vols., neatly put up in box, $3.50, or, sold separately, as follows: —

NOISY HERBERT, and other Stories for Small Children, 50 cents.

THE R. B. R.'s: MY LITTLE NEIGHBORS, 50 cents.

BESSIE GRANT'S TREASURE, 50 cents.

A SUMMER WITH THE LITTLE GRAYS, 50 cents.

FAITH AND PATIENCE. A Story — and something more — for Boys, 75 cents.

MODESTY AND MERIT, 75 cents.

All fully and finely illustrated, and tastefully bound.

ALICE'S DREAM. A Tale of Christmas-Time. Two exquisite Illustrations by Billings. 50 cents.

A charmingly written Christmas Story, worthy the perusal of old and young.

"A tone of practical common sense and piety pervades ' Alice's Dream,' and we strongly recommend it." — *Saturday Express.*

"The story is pleasantly told, and conveys a fitting Christmas lesson of true, unselfish charity." — *Boston Journal.*

"Calculated to exercise a good and refining influence upon the hearts of the young." — *Essex Co. Dem.*

"Most excellent reading for the little folks." — *Dedham Gazette.*

"A beautiful little book."

"A charming and instructive story, full of natural incidents, and set off with the graces of a cultivated manner and the gems of moral illustration." — *Phil. City Item.*

"The story is one of much pathos, is written in a chaste and elegant style, the moral lessons it teaches of the highest and purest character." — *New Covenant, Chicago.*

"It is a book that mothers may safely place in the hands of their young daughters, because its pure and beautiful teachings could only emanate from a true Christian's heart." — *Penn. State Journal.*

"We cannot get too many such books into the hands of children." — *Hartford Religious Herald.*

FRED FREELAND ; or, The Chain of Circumstances. 75 cents.

"The story and the moral are of the very best character for the young." *Rev. C. F. Barnard.*

"Fitted to exert a salutary influence upon young minds." — *Rev. A. A. Miner.*

"We cordially recommend this finely written and instructive tale." — *Philadelphia National Argus.*

"Exceedingly interesting and instructive." — *Dover Gazette.*

"Cannot fail to interest and improve." — *Burlington Sentinel.*

'Attractive in style, and unexceptionable in matter." — *Woodstock Spirit of the Age.*

"Well conceived and happily executed." — *Boston Christian Era.*

"An excellent volume." — *Greenfield Gazette.*

"We can, with much pleasure, commend it." — *Fall River News.*

"A good book." — *Haverhill Banner.*

"Inculcating an excellent moral." — *Peterson's Magazine.*

"Quite spirited, and will be read with interest." — *Northampton Gazette.*

"The general tendency of the book is wholesome." — *Salem Observer.*

"A most attractive little volume." — *Augusta Age.*

"An absorbingly interesting story." — *School Visitor.*

Scores of other notices could be added ; but these serve to indicate the estimation in which the book is held.

It should be in every Sunday-School Library and every family.

WALKER, WISE, & CO., Publishers,

245 Washington Street, Boston.

RETURN CIRCULATION DEPARTMENT
TO ➡ 202 Main Library

LOAN PERIOD 1	2	3
HOME USE		
4	5	6

ALL BOOKS MAY BE RECALLED AFTER 7 DAYS

RENEWALS AND RECHARGES MAY BE MADE 4 DAYS PRIOR TO DUE DATE.
LOAN PERIODS ARE 1-MONTH, 3-MONTHS, AND 1-YEAR.
RENEWALS: CALL (415) 642-3405

DUE AS STAMPED BELOW

NOV 2 0 1987		
AUTO. DISC.	MAY 1 8 2008	
OCT 2 6 1987		
JAN 04 1987		
DEC 1 6 1987		
DEC 11 1992		
AUTO DISC.		
DEC 1 3 1991		
CIRCULATION		

UNIVERSITY OF CALIFORNIA, BE